Intervention

by

Alan Welch

A Jeb Cassidy Western Adventure

Published by *Alan Welch*

First published 2017
This edition 2019

Copyright © Alan Welch 2018

*Please note: This book is a work of fiction. Names, characters, places and incidents are
the product of the author's imagination or are used fictitiously, and any resemblance to
actual persons living or dead, events or locales is entirely coincidental.*

ISBN 978-1-9995543-2-3

"Evil to him who evil thinks."

- King Edward the Third of England

(Honi soit qui mal y pense – motto of the Order of the Garter)

Chapters

Chapter 1 - First Meeting

Marshal Bill Yates was thinking about going home to a warm fire and his loving wife as he sat at his desk drinking bad coffee and leafing through a wad of 'Wanted' flyers. He was fully absorbed in studying the faces of known miscreants, so he was startled when his office door banged open and his papers were blown all over the office as a young man he had never seen before entered.

Strangers were something of a rarity in the town of Yellowfork, Montana, so the marshal gave the newcomer a careful once over. Longish black hair, probably in his early twenties, handsome in a rakish way, above average height, lean and fit looking, but a bit weather-beaten, open face, cold pale-blue eyes that returned Yates' gaze steadily.

Nice looking kid, the marshal thought.

But it was his garb that made him interesting. He wore a fancy, black, wide-brimmed leather hat with silver conchos around the hatband, a calf-length, black leather duster worn open, a vivid red shirt with a black bandana at the neck and elaborately tooled boots, all expensive items and well-kept. Even more interesting were the guns; ebony handled, nickel-plated Colt Navy .36 calibre revolvers, holstered in more expensive tooled black leather, one tied down just above his right knee and the other mounted in a cross-draw position just forward of his left hip.

This ain't no cowhand, Yates speculated as the young man approached his desk with his hand extended in formal greeting.

"Howdy, Marshal," the stranger greeted him as they shook hands. "Name's Jeb Cassidy and I need your help and advice."

"Well that's a first son," the middle-aged, greying marshal responded. "Most people come in here to complain about something, usually other people and their shenanigans. Take a seat and tell me, what can I help you with?"

Cassidy settled into the ladder-back chair opposite the marshal, hooked his left boot onto his right knee and sat back in a relaxed posture before replying.

"Well, sir, I am a gunfighter by profession, gunfighter not gunslinger, if you understand the distinction."

"I believe I do, but why don't you give me your take on it, so I am sure we'll be talkin' about the same thing."

" I mostly get hired by good people who are not fighters to protect them from two-legged predators, unlike a gunslinger, who just shoots whoever he is pointed at."

"Okay, young fella, that tallies pretty well with my understanding, and I assume that means I ain't gonna find your face in this bunch of flyers?" Yates riffled the stack of flyers as he said this.

"No, sir, you won't, but I need your advice so I won't end up on one of those by trying to do the right thing!" Cassidy asserted.

"Okay, let's hear it then," the veteran marshal encouraged the much younger man. "But tell me first, am I gonna need that ten-gauge on the wall over there?" He nodded in the direction of a long, wide-bored, double-barrelled shotgun in a gun rack to his right.

Cassidy glanced over to the gun rack. When his eyes came back to the marshal he found himself staring down the barrel of a cocked Colt Army.

He smiled easily. "A forty-four. Nice gun. Not a trusting man, are you, Marshal?"

"No, son, I'm not. That's why I have lived to the grand old age of forty-eight."

"Forty-eight? Gee, I thought you were older than that," grinning.

"Don't bait a man with a gun in your face, boy!"

"No, sir, I do believe that you might have a point there. But to answer your original question, no, you won't need the ten-gauge, leastwise, not on account of me."

He paused to smile at Yates then continued, "But if you did you would never have made it."

"You just saw it with your own eyes, boy. I'm still pretty damned quick."

"Yes, sir, you are. But can I show you something?"

"Sure. What?"

"Place your pistol on the desk in front of you and put your gun hand down flat next to it."

"Now why in Hell's name would I want to do a fool thing like that?"

"Come on, Marshal, trust me. I mean you no harm. I came to you for help. And this little demonstration is pertinent."

"Pertinent? You sure do like them ten dollar words, don't you, son? But, yeah, for some strange reason I do trust you. You seem like a man of your word. So here we go." With that Yates laid his big revolver down on the wood and placed his right hand alongside it.

He saw nothing discernible, just a slight blurring in his vision, before registering that he was now looking down the barrel of his own gun. The kid, in a blur of motion, cocked it, uncocked it, spun it in his hand, lifted the marshal's gun hand with his left hand and gently deposited the butt of the pistol into it with his right.

"Holy Mary, Mother of God," Yates blasphemed loudly. "I've never seen anybody move that fast in my life! You make me look like a slowpoke, and I ain't!"

"Yes, sir. No, sir. And, it's kinda why I am in the business I am in, which is why it is pertinent to what I am about to tell you."

"Well, come on then, boy, you've certainly got my interest now. And you can stop calling me sir, it makes me feel about a hunnerd. Name's Bill, Bill Yates."

"Yes, sir, er, um, Bill. I figured you *were* a hundred, but my bad." This was delivered with a disarming smile and followed by; "I will be happy to call you Bill, sir, if you will just stop calling me boy. I already told you my name is Jeb."

"You got yourself a deal, son. I will just have to remember not to offer you hard liquor." This sally elicited a guffaw from Cassidy, which in turn caused Yates to smile.

Chapter 2 - The Problem

"Let's get to it, then," the marshal prompted.

"Yeah, well, two days ago I was over in Dustbowl..."

"That town's called Dustin, kid, er, Jeb," Yates interjected.

"Yeah, but Dustbowl fits better," Cassidy answered, before continuing, "...when I had a little run-in with a few local roughnecks. No blood was spilled, I just pulled down on them and that was enough to turn them white. But afterwards I was approached in the saloon by a local rancher who had seen my speed in the face-off. He wanted to hire me. I told him that I was a gunfighter, but it seems that this fella did not know the fine distinction like you did. It turns out that he wants to hire me to murder a man, his wife and their three kids."

"God damn. Did this piece of dog vomit have a name?" Yates growled.

"Sheridan Buchanan," the gunfighter volunteered.

"Oh, Christ on a crutch," Yates moaned.

"What? You know him?" Cassidy asked in a surprised tone.

"Everybody who is from around here knows him, son. He is the biggest landowner in these parts owns a couple of hundred thousand acres, all the land around this town in fact, a huge spread, plus a bunch of businesses, lumber mills, mines, freight lines, what all else. Calls his ranch the Lazy-B, which I've always found kinda amusing. But he ain't a funny guy, no sir, he ain't. Who does he want kilt?"

"Another rancher called Avery."

"Sheeit! I know Tom Avery, too. He's a small-time rancher, only about a thousand acres, but with a sweet-water lake and a river running through it. Lots of lush grazing, trees for shade, good soil. It's a real pretty place in a sheltered valley, kind of place I would like myself one day. He raises horses, mighty fine horses, is what he does. Got a few steers too, but just for his own table and to sell a few in town here like, to help out, you know?"

"So, if he is small-time, why does Buchanan want him dead?"

"I don't really know, I am just guessing, but the history is that Avery's peaceful little valley used to be open range and Buchanan counted it as his. He used to water his stock at that sweet-water lake and on the river, and his cows grew fat on all that sweet grass. When the government started giving out land grants Buchanan didn't pay attention at the start. He just thought because everything had always been his it always would be, but it never really had been his. It was just open range. So the first Buchanan knew that Avery had filed a claim on the valley was when he started building his house. Things have been headed downhill ever since. Buchanan filed on the rest of his property right away, but he was too late for the valley. Still, I wouldn't have thought it was a killing matter. How did you leave it with Buchanan?"

"I told him I would think about it and give him an answer real soon, then lit out pronto."

"And he just let you walk out?"

"I was outta there before he had a chance to think about it, Marshal."

"Sometimes dumb luck works best," Yates observed with a grin.

There was a short pause in the conversation as both men mulled over what they had learned, then Cassidy abruptly blurted out what was uppermost in his mind.

"Does Buchanan own you, Marshal?" he asked bluntly. "He seems to own everything else around here."

Yates leaned back in his chair with a cold smile, staring straight into Cassidy's eyes, and snarled: "For someone who came here looking for help, *boy*, you sure seem to be going out of your way to piss me off!"

Cassidy held up both hands, palms out, in a gesture of surrender.

"I apologize unreservedly, Marshal," Cassidy offered. "I had to ask, under the circumstances, but I didn't think it was the case, I just needed to be sure."

Yates' smile began to thaw. "And you're sure now are you? You don't think I am that good a liar?"

"With all due respect, sir, I don't think anyone could fake that kind of deadly, righteous anger."

Now Yates was showing a completely genuine smile. "Unreservedly? With all due respect? Where the hell did you get educated, son?"

Cassidy knew he was back on safe ground when he heard the use of the word 'son' again.

"Back east, Bill, when I was young," he replied in a conciliatory tone.

"Hell, kid, you are still young," Yates ribbed him. "So you've told me what the problem is, what do you need my help and advice with?"

"What to do about it, Bill. How to handle it," Cassidy answered.

"Well, Tom Avery's valley is three or four miles outta town. My jurisdiction ends at the town limits, so I can't do any marshalling out there. About all I can do is warn Tom."

"Yes sir, I knew that coming in. I figured I don't have any jurisdictional problems, so I would handle it myself if I could. I reckon I need you to give me any information that you can on Buchanan and to introduce me to Avery, to vouch for me."

"Jesus, son, I can surely do both those things for you, but you have done bit off more than you can chew. Buchanan must have thirty, mebbe forty, hands on that ranch o' his, and they all carry guns!"

"Well, Marshal, that's a lot, but are they gun-hands or cowhands?"

"Cowhands, but what the hell does that matter? It's still thirty, forty guns. You got a death wish?"

"No, Bill, I surely don't. I intend to live through this."

"You wanted my advice, son? This is it. Don't do it."

"I have to, Marshal. Now that I know about it I could not live with myself if I let this bastard Buchanan roll over, murder, an entire family."

"If you go ahead, son, you sure as hell ain't going to have to worry about living with yourself!" the Marshal snarled.

That brought a smile to the young man's face. "Well, Bill, I guess I would be one less thing for you to fret about then," he said.

"You know, young Jeb, I admire your guts and your integrity, but I as sure as cussing ain't admiring your smarts," Yates growled.

"Never did claim to be smart," Cassidy answered, grinning at him.

"We agree on one thing at least, then," the marshal retorted, standing. "Come on, son. You're coming to supper with me. My Mary is a right good cook and she dearly loves company, even ornery saddle tramps like you."

Cassidy rose, thanking the older man for his hospitality and expressing his pleasure at the honour.

"Save the soft soap for Mary, Jeb. She'll lap it up. Me, I ain't your mother."

That caused Cassidy to grin from ear to ear. "No, Marshal, you surely ain't," he agreed.

"And don't say ain't just because I say ain't. I'll have your hide."

"No, sir," with mock chagrin from Cassidy, then "Ornery old cuss, aren't you, sir?"

Yates uttered an involuntary guffaw, struggled to convert it into a cough, then gave up and grinned at the youngster. "You're alright, kid," he said.

"Thank you, Bill, that means a lot," Cassidy responded sincerely, feeling that he had found a friend and ally in the older man.

Chapter 3 - The Plan

At the marshal's cozy house on the edge of town Cassidy was introduced to Mary and made welcome. She was a pleasant looking woman a few years younger than her husband and, as Yates had predicted, she was delighted to have company. While Mary bustled about the kitchen and the men drank coffee at the kitchen table Yates explained Cassidy's predicament to her.

When she had heard him out Mary turned to Cassidy and explained to him in no uncertain terms that she would rather be serving dinner to a healthy young man next week than attending his funeral. Cassidy quailed slightly before the onslaught, then was shocked when the woman pulled him into a hug.

"Don't mind me, lad," she apologized. "I am just a mother hen. I understand that you are going to do what you think is right. Just know that if you get hurt, or just if you need it, we will take care of you here for as long as it takes."

Cassidy was so surprised by her kindness that he felt his throat choke up and found himself unable to speak for a few seconds. Finally he managed to get some words out. "Thank you for your kindness, ma'am. I sincerely hope that I will not have to be a bother to you."

"No bother, Jeb. You will always be welcome here," she assured him.

Conversation was light during the very pleasant meal, after which Jeb and the marshal adjourned to the living room with steaming cups of coffee to discuss the matter at hand. Yates searched his memory for recollections of the Lazy-B cowhands that he had met and came up with twenty-nine.

"There are probably a few that I don't know, and a few will have moved on, so I think thirty is a fair guess," he told Cassidy. "The one to watch out for in particular is his foreman, Jack Scranton. He is a big, ugly bastard with a thick black beard and a large scar next to his right eye. He's a mean son of a bitch, all the hands are scared of him. I hear tell that he beat one of his men to death with his bare hands over some small insult, but no body ever turned up, none of the other hands would talk about it, so I could never prove it even happened. I believe it, though. If it gets ugly, don't let that brute get his hands on you, son."

"I won't, Bill. If this goes down ugly I expect it to be a shooting war. My big question for you is, how can I get some kind of legal status for this, so I don't end up on the end of a rope or the most wanted man in Montana, if

Buchanan or his boys put their own version of things into powerful ears before I can?"

"Well, I am going to deputize you before we head out to Avery's place, so that star on your chest should at least give some people pause. But like I already explained, I don't got no jurisdiction out there, so it's more for show than anything, it won't protect you from Buchanan. He knows the law, even if he don't respect it. But, right now, circuit Judge Palmer happens to be in town and he is a good man. I reckon I can get him to appoint you as a county sheriff if we tell him what's up. That should stop anybody stretching your neck, if you should live that long!"

"I thought you already had a county sheriff?" queried Cassidy.

"We do, but he's a runaway cat and I don't see why we can't have two. Judge Palmer don't mind bending the rules from time to time in a good cause, and he'll sure as shooting see preventing the murders of a family of five as a good cause," the marshal assured Cassidy.

The two men then went on to discuss the details of the terrain surrounding the Avery ranch and the nature of Sheridan Buchanan, who Yates portrayed as a typical ruthless, loud-mouthed bully who had accumulated sufficient wealth to wield tremendous power in his immediate surroundings, enabling him to ride roughshod over his neighbours, but without any connections to men of real power and influence at the state level.

"There won't be any cavalry coming to his rescue, or any lynch mob looking to avenge him, if' you should happen to shoot the son of a bitch dead," he predicted. "So you will only have to fight the army he has with him, if it comes down to it. So, just thirty-two guns or thereabouts, counting Buchanan and his foreman. No worries, eh, lad?" he finished sarcastically.

"Which brings me to the other thing I need your help with, Bill," Cassidy responded, ignoring the sarcasm completely. "Some logistical difficulties."

"Them being what specifically?" Yates asked.

"Guns and ammunition, Bill. If this turns into a major gunfight I can't be having to reload all the time or I will get dead in a hurry! You know how slow and careful you have to be loading these cap-and-ball revolvers, and I could get shot full of holes while I am doing it. I need you to lend me as many pistols as you can rustle up and a couple of Winchesters if you have them. And ammunition for all those guns. I have the two pistols I am wearing and two more in my saddle bags, plus my Winchester saddle-gun. So that's a total of thirty-six rounds before I have to reload. I need at least twice that."

"What, you can't get her done with thirty-six shots?" the marshal asked mockingly.

Cassidy grinned at the jibe. "No, sir, I am good, but I *ain't* that good!"

Yates chuckled and said, "Give me a minute," as he rose from his chair and headed upstairs. Returning in a few minutes he handed Cassidy a large brass-bound walnut case as he sat back down.

The younger man opened the box curiously, his eyes widening as he saw what was within. Two beautifully engraved Remington single-action revolvers lay on a red velvet bed. They had a rich blued finish, the barrels and frames were inlaid with silver oak leaves, and the grips were mother of pearl.

"Wow, Bill, these are beautiful," Cassidy enthused.

"Yeah, they were a gift from the citizens of Abilene, the previous place I marshalled, after I prevented a bank robbery. They're forty-fours, so you will find they kick more than your thirty-sixes, but they are real accurate. So don't get yerself kilt; I want them back," Yates growled. "I've got two more Colt Armys in my desk drawers. You can have them, too. Oh, and you can borrow the ten-gauge from the office as well. I've found that quietens down would-be tough guys real quick."

"That should about do it, Bill, thanks."

"You can stay here tonight and we will pick up the other guns in the morning. Then I'll take you out to meet the Avery's," Yates offered.

Chapter 4 - Enlightenment

Rising early the next morning, Cassidy enjoyed a home-cooked breakfast prepared by Mary, a real pleasure for him as he experienced it so infrequently. He and the marshal then headed into the marshal's office to pick up the promised guns, after Cassidy had thanked Mary profusely for her hospitality and great cooking. At the office Yates explained the situation to his deputy, a young, amiable blond man named Callum McGuthrie, asking him to round up three more young men to act as deputies for the duration of the impending confrontation. Before heading out to recruit a few of his friends the deputy produced two more spare revolvers that he graciously loaned to Cassidy.

Taking the ten-gauge shotgun from the wall rack and tossing it to Cassidy the marshal said, "Shells are in the desk drawer. Let's go see the judge, see if we can make you some kind of legal."

Helping himself to a box of ammunition from the drawer, Cassidy asked' "Do you think he'll go for it?"

"Yes, I do," the marshal averred. "He purely hates murdering scum and pretty much believes in taking 'em down any way you can, an attitude that has helped me out a few times over the years. You can clean up a town pretty quick with a judge like that around."

"Guess so," Cassidy replied with a laugh.

The judge was in his informal office when they arrived – a back table in the saloon. The saloon itself became a courtroom when needed.

When Yates had finished explaining the situation to the judge, laying great emphasis on Sheridan Buchanan's plans to murder not only Tom Avery but his wife and three daughters as well, the judge looked Cassidy over carefully before observing, "You seem in an awful hurry to die for one so young, son."

Cassidy chuckled. "No, sir, I don't plan to die doing this. I am just not going to let it happen."

"Good for you, young man, we could do with more like you," the judge responded, then turning to Yates asked, "What are you going to do about Avery and his family?"

"Tom's a reasonable man, Judge," answered the marshal. "I am going to bring him and his womenfolk into town, house them in the jail and surround them with me and four deputies until this is over."

"Get yourself another six deputies if you can. I will have the county pay for them. You will need more guns if this young fella gets himself killed," the judge directed the marshal. Cassidy shook his head dismissively.

"I'm not sure I can find that many as will want to get involved in a shooting war, Judge, but I will try, and thank you," responded Yates.

"As for you, young fella," the judge said, turning to Cassidy, "Let's turn you into a county sheriff. Raise your right hand and repeat after me..."

When he was duly sworn in, the judge asked the marshal to supply a badge, as he did not carry those around with him.

Handing Cassidy a star, Yates told him, "It's a town marshal's star, but that don't matter. The judge and I are witnesses that you were sworn as a county sheriff, so you are covered. If you live your actions will be legal, if you are dead the law, that's me and the judge here, will make sure Buchanan pays for it. Oh, and we'll make sure you are buried proper."

"Well, I am sure my corpse will be duly grateful, Marshal," Cassidy replied with a cocksure grin.

Yates frowned, but the judge guffawed. "I remember what it was like to be young and think that you could never die," he observed.

With his frown turning to a wry smile, Yates said, "Okay, son, let's go get the Avery family. You can be my bodyguard on the way!"

Cassidy was still laughing as they mounted up and rode out.

It was a short ride across scrubby country to reach the Avery spread, their horses trailing dust most of the way, but as they entered the lower end of the hidden valley it was like entering a different world. Small hills, only a couple of hundred feet high, enclosed the valley; the slopes were heavily wooded, while the valley floor was covered with lush grass rising almost to the bellies of the two men's horses. A good-sized river meandered through the centre, down through a series of railed paddocks containing hundreds of fine-looking horses, to curve past the eastern side of a large frame ranch-house with a covered porch on three sides in the middle distance, painted white and gleaming in the bright sunshine. A large lake could be seen at the far end of the valley

Reining in to admire the sight, Cassidy said, "I can see why you admire this place, Marshal. I would like something like this myself one day."

"Yeah, it's a grand place, ain't it? The Avery's are fine people, too. It's a good thing you are doing, son," Yates replied.

Embarrassed by the praise Cassidy spurred his horse into a trot and set off towards the house. As he approached, a lean middle-aged man with a rifle crooked in his arm walked out onto the porch, alerted by the sound of hooves, to gaze in his direction. Recognizing the marshal behind Cassidy, he leaned the rifle against a porch post and waved in greeting. Yates waved back and shortly thereafter the two riders reined in before the porch.

"Howdy, Tom," Yates greeted the rancher, "Need to talk to you about summat important. Mind if we step down."

"Go ahead, Bill," answered Tom Avery. "Turn your horses loose in the small paddock at the side of the house and come right in."

Upon entering the house Cassidy was introduced to Avery, his wife Emily and his three daughters, the oldest of whom was, Cassidy guessed, around eighteen years old and quite the prettiest young lady he had ever seen. He had a hard job tearing his eyes away as he was led off to the large, comfortably furnished living room to discuss the reason for their presence with the rancher and his wife. The marshal summed up the situation as briefly as possible before explaining that he was proposing to take the family back to town with him for their own protection and that Cassidy would stay behind to deal with the Buchanan threat.

The marshal then asked Avery if he had any idea why Buchanan might want him and his family dead, whether it was simply greed for the fine land and water that their ranch occupied or if there was something else at the bottom of it.

"Well, Bill, I suspect it goes back a ways further than that," the rancher replied.

He then went on to explain that he and his wife Emily had grown up together in a small town in Virginia. Buchanan had also lived there, although he was a few years older, so they had not known each other well. In the summer of the year in which Tom and Emily had turned twenty years of age the town had held a barn dance, to which just about everybody in town and from the surrounding ranches had come to have some fun. Emily, being young and very pretty, was asked to dance by many young men, among whom were both Tom Avery and Sheridan Buchanan. She had danced with each of them several times, but her heart belonged to Avery, although he did not know it yet, so in the latter part of the evening she spent all her time dancing with him.

Buchanan had been drinking and, after Emily refused his invitation to dance for the third time, he grabbed her by the arm and pulled her roughly onto the dance floor. Emily protested loudly, drawing Tom's attention. He promptly intervened, wrenching Buchanan's fingers from Emily's arm and telling him to get the hell away from her. Unsurprisingly, Buchanan threw a punch at Tom's head, which he ducked, then Tom delivered a cross to Buchanan's jaw that dropped him to the floor. Roaring with rage, Buchanan leaped to his feet and tried to tackle Tom to the ground. Tom side-stepped, delivering a rabbit punch to the neck as Buchanan bulled through the empty space, dropping him to the ground once more. This time, as he rose to his feet, Buchanan pulled his pistol with murderous intent, but Tom was faster, stepping in close and twisting the gun from his hand before Buchanan could cock it, then slamming the butt into his temple, knocking the raging drunk out cold.

Avery had then dragged the unconscious man outside and dunked his head repeatedly in a horse trough until he recovered consciousness. Buchanan then staggered to his feet, hauled himself bodily into the saddle aboard his horse and rode out of town, never to be seen again.

"So, imagine my surprise," Avery went on, "When twenty-some years later, having just moved my family out here and built this place, I see Buchanan coming out of the saloon as I am going into the general store for supplies. He saw me, too. I asked the storekeeper about him and got the bad news that not only was he the richest man in these parts but he was also my nearest neighbour. I have been waiting for something bad to happen ever since, but have been hoping that he might have changed."

"Well, that might explain him wanting to bust you up some," Yates reasoned, "But murdering you and your entire family? It don't make sense."

"I have a wrangler works for me, off and on, helping out with the horses," Avery volunteered. "He told me a while back that Buchanan had been heavy into the whisky one night in the saloon and he got maudlin. He was telling his foreman how it was my fault that he had never married, that I stole the only woman he had ever cared for, that my wife should have been his wife and that my kids should have been his kids. Seems he has rewritten the past in his head so that I am the cause of all his unhappiness, whatever that might be."

"It's all utter rubbish, Bill," Emily protested. "He never had a chance with me, it was always Tom. But the fool man has talked himself into it and now he hates Tom for something that never was!"

"Well, Em," Yates replied, "The reasons don't matter much no more. He's in a killing mind and we have to deal with that, so kindly pack up your necessaries and get ready to move into town for a short while until this is done."

"Yeah, that'd be good, Em," Avery backed the marshal. "But I think I should stay and help the lad here. Can't have him fighting my battles on his own-some."

"If you don't mind, sir, I'd prefer that you go into town with the marshal," Cassidy interjected.

Looking surprised and ready for an argument, Avery responded, "Call me Tom, son. You're risking your life for my family so we should be on first name terms. And why would you want to turn down my help?"

"Because it won't be a help to me, Tom" Cassidy demurred. "There are going to be a whole passel of guns out there. If it gets down to gun-play and I am on my own I can just shoot anything that moves. If you are here I have to know where you are at all times and try to avoid shooting you by accident. That will slow me down and could get me killed. Please go with the marshal."

"Huh. That's about the only argument you could have used that would convince me, son. But don't you get yourself killed or I will have to tan your hide!" Avery said, deferring to the younger man's judgment.

"I don't plan to, Tom, and I wish people would stop bringing it up. You all might jinx me!" Cassidy replied testily.

Emily laughed. "At least let me feed you, then," she offered. "You might as well fight on a full stomach, if you have to."

"That would be great, ma'am," Cassidy accepted. "I sure do like home cooking."

Emily laughed again. "You and every other young man I know," she remarked.

"Hey, us old 'uns appreciate it, too," her husband objected, causing laughter all round.

Chapter 5 - Confrontation

After a companionable meal it took about an hour to load the wagon with the necessary clothing and provisions for the family's stay in town. Yates had explained that they would be staying in the jail, where they could be protected by heavily armed men, so bedding was also included in the load. Emily told Cassidy to make free use of their home, but he politely informed them that, though he might avail himself of some victuals, he would be making his camp in the woods, where he would be harder to find if anybody came looking. The Avery's made their farewells to Cassidy, thanking him profusely and wishing him well, then headed out in the direction of Yellowfork.

The marshal hung back for a brief talk with Cassidy before following them.

"I'll keep them safe, don't you worry, lad," he told Cassidy. "What's your next move?"

"I know you will, Bill. I am going to let Buchanan know that I won't be doing his dirty work and that I am now a county sheriff, see if I can provoke him into doing something stupid," Cassidy informed him.

"Whatever else he is, he ain't stupid," Yates advised. "Take care."

"Always, Marshal," Cassidy replied, grinning.

"Yeah, sure. Fool kid," the marshal rejoined, but he was also grinning. "If'n I don't hear from you inside three days I will be coming out here with as many good men as I can raise, and to hell with what's legal and what ain't!"

"That's the stuff, Marshal," Cassidy said approvingly, clapping him on the shoulder. "Make sure you've got plenty of guns around you at the jail, too, in case that bastard gets word they are there and comes visiting."

"I'll get her done and I'll see you soon," Yates replied, then mounted up and headed after the wagon.

Cassidy mounted up and rode his horse into the woods to the West of the ranch, working his way through the widely spaced trees to the top of the low hill, where he paused to take in what could be seen from this vantage point. He knew that Buchanan's Lazy-B ranch lay due West along the wide trail that he could see curving around the base of the hill and discovered that from this height he could observe anyone approaching along the trail from a mile or so away, which would give him adequate warning of any impending raid. Satisfied, he spurred his big chestnut gelding down the far slope and onto the trail.

After riding for an hour through a rolling terrain of rough grass and large boulders he came to the gate to Buchanan's spread, a tall, open pole gateway with the name "Lazy-B" and the brand burned into a ten-foot board spanning the entrance. As Cassidy turned in he could see a very large ranch-house, surrounded by several corrals, about a half-mile distant. Trotting towards the house Cassidy noted a wrangler working a pony in the corral closest to the building, a cowhand sitting on the steps of the bunkhouse, which was off to his left, cleaning a saddle, and two riders hazing a small group of cattle into a distant pen. Only the riders appeared to be armed.

Seeing a man emerge from the house on to the wide, shaded front porch when he was some twenty paces from the house, Cassidy reined in and called a greeting: "Hello, the house."

The figure on the porch stepped from the shadow into the sunlight at the front of the porch and Cassidy recognized Sheridan Buchanan. He was in shirtsleeves and was weaponless.

"Cassidy," he greeted the gunfighter, with a nod. "I take it you have an answer for me?"

"Yes, sir," Cassidy replied. "I won't be taking the work. I have found me another job."

Angry colour flooded into the rancher's face. "What? Who are you gonna be working for?"

Cassidy pulled back the lapel of his black leather duster to reveal the star pinned to his shirt.

"The county, Mister Buchanan. It appears I am County Sheriff now," Cassidy answered. "I am sure you can see where there might be what they call a conflict of interest."

"You double-dealing snake!" Buchanan roared. "Get off my land, right now!"

The angry shout brought three more cowhands out of the bunkhouse, all with guns in hand.

Tipping the brim of his hat to the irate rancher with his left hand, Cassidy said, "Glad to, Buchanan."

Switching his reins to his left hand and dropping his right close to his pistol, he backed his horse away, scanning the edgy group of cowhands carefully as he did so. When he was beyond pistol range he whirled his horse and took off at a dead run.

Didn't think that one through too good, did you, Jeb, he thought to himself as he high-tailed it.

As Cassidy disappeared from sight Buchanan turned on the ranch hands.

"Get the hell after him and make sure that he don't come back, ever!" he shouted in rage.

The four men on the bunkhouse porch jumped to do his bidding, grabbing gun-belts and running to their horses, which they lashed into a headlong gallop in pursuit of Cassidy.

The gunfighter knew that Buchanan would almost certainly send men after him so, when he came to a small rise, he reined up and circled his horse to survey his back-trail. About a mile back he saw riders coming at full gallop.

Four, he thought. *Okay.*

Wheeling his horse and taking off at a fast lope he followed the trail through a small, deep arroyo then between low, boulder-strewn cliffs, immediately after which the road took a hard turn to the left. Pulling the horse to a halt, Cassidy then swung it in a full circle, examining his surroundings carefully. The cliffs on both sides were only about twenty feet high, but they were sheer, with huge boulders in a number of places at their feet; they confined the trail for perhaps another hundred yards beyond the bend. Any rider on the road had no way to climb out once they were in the chute. Cassidy decided it was a perfect place for the first clash in his battle.

He took position about twenty-five yards on the blind side of the bend with his horse broadside across the trail, his right side towards the bend. He then leaned forward, resting his right forearm across the saddle horn, which positioned his right hand conveniently over the butt of his cross-draw Colt Navy while his body concealed any view of it. The other Colt tied down on his right leg would be exposed to the view of the approaching enemy and he was hoping that they would assume that was his only pistol and would thus focus their attention on it, giving him an edge for the unexpected cross-draw. Of course, if any of them had been paying close attention when he was in Buchanan's stable-yard this was wasted effort, but you did what you could and hoped for the best.

He only had to wait a couple of minutes before the four riders came thrashing around the bend full tilt and were forced to come to a crashing stop when they found him blocking the road. The first rider's horse reared when it was dragged to a sudden stop and almost toppled over backwards before regaining its footing, the second rider slithered to a halt with the horse's front legs extended straight out and its rear legs folded so far under that it was almost sitting, and the other two rider's pulled out to the sides, their horses sidling and prancing. Cassidy sat passively watching as they gradually regained control of their mounts.

"Looking for me, boys?" he asked when they were settled.

"Yeah, Cassidy," the lead rider replied. "The boss wants you dead."

"And he sent you?" Cassidy replied scornfully. "He should have sent more."

"Big talk, saddle-tramp," the man to Cassidy's left called over.

Cassidy sighed. "Okay, boys, let's get it done," he said.

The leader glanced around at each of his confederates, realized that they were all waiting on his lead, and turned back to Cassidy, who merely raised his eyebrows.

The cowhand made his move, grabbing for the heavy pistol at his hip, which galvanized the other three riders to reaching for their iron, too.

In one smooth, blisteringly fast motion Cassidy flipped the cross-draw, cocked and fired straight into the leaders face, then fanned the hammer to take down the other three riders. All four men pitched from their saddles without ever getting off a shot. The sulphurous stench of burned black-powder hung in the air.

Two of the men still lived. The leader was writhing on his back, making strange gurgling, choking noises; when Cassidy rode over he saw that half of the man's jaw had been blown off, but he was miraculously still breathing. The gunfighter mercifully finished him off with a bullet to the brain. Walking his horse over to the other survivor, the man who had been on his left, Cassidy saw that the cowhand was trying to hold his intestines in with both hands.

"Please, mister, kill me," the man begged, his face contorted in agony.

The gunfighter nodded. "Via con Dios, compadre," he murmured, then shot him through the forehead.

Stepping down from his horse, Cassidy examined the remaining two men, but they were both dead. Looking around at the carnage he muttered sadly, "Sorry, boys. You should have stuck to cow punching."

He painstakingly reloaded his now empty Colt, then remounted and hazed his victim's horses back towards Buchanan's ranch, figuring that their return would hasten the impending confrontation. Now that he was in it, he wanted it done.

Once he had the four horses loping steadily towards their home barn he turned and headed back to the Avery place.

Chapter 6 - Nightriders

As he unrolled his saddle roll in the Avery's parlour and extracted his additional guns, he speculated that, if he was lucky, this could all be over tonight. He expected Buchanan to come after dark; it was in the nature of the man, and evil deeds were usually done under cover of night. Failing tonight, it could be a long, indefinite wait.

Laying out his weapons on the floor, Cassidy tried to work out the best way of arranging them on his person so that he could access them easily but they would not foul each other on the draw. He had a total of ten pistols, his own rifle and the marshal's ten-gauge shotgun to deploy. The rifle and shotgun were not a problem; they each had saddle boots, so he would secure the rifle under his right leg when mounted and the shotgun under his left, from where they could be quickly yanked out if needed.

They were, however, a last resort measure; he fully expected to do the majority of fighting, if it came to that, with pistols.

The two pistols that he usually wore were not an issue either; they would be holstered in their usual positions. He had a fancy shoulder rig for his other two pistols, also Colt Navy thirty-sixes, which would position them comfortably beneath his armpits for a high cross-draw. The marshal's two beautiful Remington's did not come with leather, but he found that he could tuck these under his belt at the small of his back with their butts facing out and still pull them pretty damned quick. Six.

The marshal's other two forty=fours had come with holsters, but they were both right-hand draws. Cassidy experimented and found that he could lash the gun-belts around his saddle-horn for one straight draw on the right and one cross or back-hand draw on the left, both of which were satisfactory. Eight.

That just left the deputy's two forty=fours needing a home. Cassidy realized that he was out of body options and short on gun leather, so he improvised. Hunting around the tack room in the barn he unearthed a ball of strong twine. Cutting off two generous lengths he threaded one length through the trigger of each of the remaining revolvers then mounted his horse. He then looped the cords diagonally across his chest so that one pistol rested on each side of the horse, hanging by the trigger guards. By adjusting the lengths of the cords he then positioned the pistols so that he could reach them with a quick grab behind his hips. It was not a great arrangement, but it worked and it gave him twelve more rounds without a reload. When he was satisfied that the guns were at the most convenient height he cut off the excess cord. Ten. Done.

Repacking his bedroll and tying it to the back of his saddle, the gunfighter mounted up and headed into the woods to the west of the house, where he rode to the top of the hill, tied his horse to a tree and settled down on a convenient log to watch the road.

The day was warm, the shade was pleasant and Cassidy was comfortable on his log with his back against a tree. After a while his head began to nod down to his chest and he jerked awake suddenly several times before dropping into a peaceful doze. When he was startled awake by the thunder of hooves it was pitch dark. Shaking his head to rouse himself, he peered towards the road and saw a dozen or so flaming torches spread throughout a group of maybe thirty night-riders in flour sack hoods trotting briskly along the trail right at the foot of the hill.

Cursing softly to himself, Cassidy untied his horse, vaulted into the saddle and made his way hurriedly down through the trees on the far side of the hill. He intersected the trail about a hundred yards ahead of the bunched up night-riders, reining in while still hidden within the trees, allowing the riders to close the distance before revealing himself. As he waited he made the decision to use the pistols suspended by cords first; he wanted pistols already in hand when he braced the mob and it made sense to use the corded revolvers for this as it would remove the necessity for groping around for them later when the action heated up. Taking one revolver in each hand he urged his chestnut from the trees into the centre of the trail when the approaching riders were twenty paces or so distant, guiding the animal with his knees.

"This is a joke, right, Buchanan?" he called to the hooded man riding a big pinto stallion at the front of the tightly bunched riders, who were now all pulling to a hasty stop.

"What?" the rider shouted back.

"I mean, you're riding that big pinto that you always ride, you're wearing the same clothes you were wearing when I saw you in town, every damn horse in this bunch is wearing your brand, and you think people won't recognize you because you put a flour sack over your head? It has to be a joke, no?" Cassidy taunted.

The lead rider tore off his hood and tossed it to the road. "Alright, Cassidy, so you know who we are. So what? Get the hell out of my way!" Buchanan challenged.

Following Buchanan's lead the other riders began tossing their hoods to the ground, obviously glad to be rid of the sweaty, smelly confinement.

"Just making conversation, Buchanan," Cassidy returned politely. "Where you headed?"

Buchanan pondered the question while glaring at Cassidy, decided there was no reason to deny him an answer, and said shortly, "The Avery place."

"They aren't there," the gunfighter informed him.

"We'll see," Buchanan responded in obvious disbelief, nudging his horse into a walk towards Cassidy.

"No, you won't," Cassidy asserted, turning his horse sideways across the road and blocking Buchanan's path.

Buchanan halted his horse once more, clearly indecisive, wary of the gunfighter's skills, but the large, black-bearded man to his right with the scarred face sidled his horse to the right, so that the barrel of the Winchester that was resting on his saddle-horn aligned itself with Cassidy's gut, and said, "Move, mister, or I'll blow you to hell."

Cassidy glanced at the man, stone faced. "You must be Jack Scranton?" he queried.

The bearded man grinned widely. "See, boys," he called to the group of riders, "I'm famous!"

"No, you're not," Cassidy contradicted. "The marshal just told me to watch out for an ugly bastard with a black beard and a scar."

Then he shot him in the throat.

The movement was so fast that none of the assembled riders saw Cassidy's pistol swing in Scranton's direction, but they all saw the spurt of blood as the ball entered the foreman's throat below his chin, the eruption of blood, brain matter and bone fragments as it severed the spinal cord and blew out the base of the skull, the horrified expressions of the riders behind who were liberally splattered with the gory mess, and the blank expression on the face of the corpse as it slid over the back of the saddle, down the right flank of the horse and thudded to the ground with its right foot caught in the stirrup. The frightened horse shied to its right and took of across the meadow in front of the Avery's house at a panicked gallop, dragging the lifeless body behind.

The tableau froze for a moment, then chaos ensued as horses, panicked by the gunshot and the smell of blood, reared, pranced, bucked and shuffled while their riders fought to control them. A rider to the rear shouted to Buchanan, "I didn't sign up for this, boss! I ain't getting kilt for no twenty bucks a month!" and whirled his pony away, spurring it back up the trail, away from the gunfighter's threatening guns. Ten or twelve other riders immediately followed him, high-tailing it up the road in a cloud of dust.

Well, Cassidy thought, *that cut down the numbers a mite.* But there were still twenty or so left.

The remaining riders scattered around Cassidy, pulling their pistols and opening fire. One ball whined past his ear and Cassidy realized he had best start moving, to make himself a harder target. He spurred his horse forward through the group still on the trail, firing with both hands as he rode. Both guns were empty when he burst through the rear of the group and turned his horse to the left to begin a circling movement. He was a better shot with his right hand than with his left, but he remembered emptying four saddles with the right gun and three with the left, so the odds were getting better.

Dropping the corded pistols and allowing them to swing free, he pulled the two forty=fours from the holsters lashed to his saddle-horn and started picking off individual riders as he circled the perimeter of the milling bunch. Three more riders fell before they began to panic and flee. Seeing the first two riders turn tail and run Cassidy felt exultant, but then he recognized the big paint stallion and realized that Buchanan was leading the rout. This was not over yet!

Pulling his horse to a standstill Cassidy caught his breath, letting his horse blow, and did a swift count of the fleeing night-riders. Eleven.

I certainly thinned them out a bit, he thought with an inner satisfied smile.

Chapter 7 - Showdown

S urveying the battleground he saw a dense cloud of black-powder smoke hovering over the part of the road where most of the shooting had taken place and dissipating slowly as a gentle breeze wafted it apart. The night was dark and still as he urged the chestnut into a walk and rode to check the scattered bodies. None lived. Relaxing, he unhooked the empty corded revolvers from around his chest and stuffed them into his saddlebags, but as he did so was suddenly alarmed by the disturbing idea that Buchanan might not be simply fleeing back to the Lazy-B as he had assumed.

Kicking the chestnut into a fast lope he sped through the trees to the top of the westerly hill, reining in at the top to eye the dark road. In the distance he could see the glow of the blazing torches carried by the fleeing riders. Knowing that there was a fork in the road ahead of them, the west branch of which led past Buchanan's ranch and the south branch of which led to town, Cassidy sat quietly watching to see which way the riders went. When after a few minutes he saw the distant lights veer left onto the south branch he hissed "Shit!" between his teeth and sent the chestnut hurtling down the slope of the hill in pursuit, trusting the intelligent creature to avoid tree trunks and other obstacles in the darkness. Reaching the trail without mishap he put the horse into a full gallop and hoped that he could catch up to Buchanan and his men in time to do some good, knowing full well that Buchanan must have guessed the whereabouts of the Avery family and would be intent on wresting them from the marshal's protection.

Racing through the southern fork in the road towards town Cassidy saw no sign of the night-riders before he reached the town's outskirts. Reining his horse down to a lope as he entered the main street, he saw the riders clustered at the far end in front of the marshal's office and jail, illuminated by their burning brands. Dismounting fifty yards away, he threw his reins over a hitching rail and took to the boardwalk running along the store frontages. Striding towards the tightly grouped riders he was amazed that nobody appeared to have noticed his arrival. The riders were still in the process of forming a line across the frontage of the marshal's office, so they had obviously only just beaten him here.

While still thirty yards away Cassidy heard Buchanan shout, "Give me Avery, Marshal, and you can walk away."

"Oh, I don't think so, Buchanan," Yates called back. "Even if I believed you, which I don't, I figure that man and his family would be dead about ten seconds after I came out, and me and my deputies with them. I reckon I'll just stay behind these nice stone walls and blow you to hell!"

"Come out or I'll burn you out!" roared Buchanan.

"Stone don't burn, ass-hole," Yates shouted back.

"Roofs do," Buchanan returned, motioning to one of his men to throw his torch onto the roof.

As the man drew his arm back to throw Cassidy called out, "Hey, boys, you left the party early!"

Many of the riders instinctively swung their horses towards the sound of his voice, including the torch thrower. Cassidy drew his right Colt, cocked and fired in one smooth blur of motion, nailing the torch thrower in the centre of his chest, blowing him from the saddle, the torch flying from his hand and hitting the dusty street just before his inert body.

Cassidy then tracked his pistol along the line of riders from right to left, fanning the hammer and seeing blood spurt from five more riders, but miraculously none fell from their horses as they milled in confusion.

Slamming the empty Colt back into its holster, Cassidy cross-drew its mate as a fusillade of fire broke out from the windows of the marshal's office. Somewhere in his consciousness Cassidy registered three rifles and a shotgun as he was bringing his pistol to bear. The more powerful long guns brought down three riders to his left, one of whom was missing most of his face and the top of his head, presumably the target of the shotgun.

Moving his gaze past the already dead men Cassidy was confronted by the sight of Buchanan's big pinto bulling its way through the other riders directly at him. As it registered he saw Buchanan levelling his pistol at him and instinctively fired straight into the man's rage-contorted face, then fanned the hammer to empty the pistol into his chest.

Buchanan's lifeless body lurched over the left side of his horse's neck and pitched face down into the dust of the roadway, only to be trampled by the hooves of a riderless pony as it fled the gunfire..

Cassidy dodged behind a support post on the boardwalk as he holstered the thirty-six and pulled the marshal's two fancy Remington's from the small of his back.

Yelling, "Marshal! Cease fire!" in the hope that this might prevent the marshal or his deputies from accidentally shooting him, he stepped out into the street, dodging between the horses and blowing riders from their saddles at point-blank range with both hands. Riderless horses were scattering from him in all directions as he finally came to a standstill in the centre of the street, turning in a circle with both pistols levelled, searching for targets, but there were none. An eerie quiet settled on the street, broken by the creaking of the jail door opening as Yates stepped out, shotgun in hand.

Gazing cautiously around at the bodies littered all over the main street, the marshal approached the slightly dazed-looking Cassidy warily. Stepping in close he gently pushed the barrels of the gunfighter's pistols down with his left hand, saying soothingly, "It's alright, son. We're done. It's over."

Cassidy's eyes snapped back into focus and turned towards Yates.

"How many, Bill?" he asked, nodding towards the corpses.

Yates did a quick body count and replied, "Eleven, Jeb."

Cassidy sighed. "That's all of them then. It really is over," he pronounced with evident relief.

"What about the rest of his men?" the marshal enquired. "Surely you didn't kill them all?"

"No, not all of them," Cassidy answered heavily. "Ten or twelve of them lit out after I killed Scranton. You'll find another ten of them close to Avery's place and maybe four more on the trail to Buchanan's ranch, unless he picked them up himself."

"You killed them all?" Yates asked incredulously.

"Yeah, dead," Cassidy responded tiredly.

"Yeah, well, that's how they usually end up when you kill 'em, son," the marshal observed wryly, slipping an arm over the gunfighter's shoulders and walking him towards his office. "Let's have a drink to settle you down and you can tell us what happened," he suggested.

Chapter 8 - Aftermath

Entering the marshal's office Cassidy was greeted first by the marshal's regular deputy Callum McGuthrie, who slapped him on the back and told him that he had never seen shooting like that and bet that he never would again, and then by five strangers who had been deputized for the emergency. As he was being introduced, Tom Avery and his family emerged from the cells out back and joined the celebratory group. Avery shook Cassidy's hand warmly and told him that he would be forever grateful for what Cassidy had done for his family and that he was immensely relieved to see him alive and unharmed. His wife Emily hugged Cassidy hard and cried quietly with relief on his chest for a brief moment, before scrubbing at her eyes and declaring firmly that she would put the coffee pot on to boil.

Cassidy asked how come, with eight men in the marshal's office he had only heard four guns firing and Yates explained that the two windows were so small that only two shooters could fire from each of them at the same time without fouling each others aim, so the other four men had been kept in reserve in case the enemy somehow broke into the jail.

Yates next produced several glasses and a bottle of whisky from his desk drawer and began pouring while his deputy retrieved more glasses from the tiny kitchen off to one side of the office, then got Cassidy started on relating his adventures over the last twelve hours. While he was talking and the men were sipping Emily delivered mugs of hot coffee, which chased the whisky nicely.

At the conclusion of Cassidy's narrative Yates observed, "You've had a busy night, son. Are you okay?"

"Yeah, mostly, I guess, Bill," the younger man answered. "But it all seems so, I dunno, unnecessary, I suppose."

"How so?" the marshal asked, frowning. "You saved the whole Avery family here."

"I know, Bill, and that makes it all worthwhile, but this was all caused by one deluded, vengeful, murderous bully and he led all these other men to their deaths over something that only existed in his crazy head!" Cassidy explained.

"Well, son," Yates rejoined, "Evil men lead good men to their deaths all the time."

"True, and those who died with him in the street here were obviously the hard core of his outfit, not good men. But those who died outside of town, except for Scranton, were not bad men; they were just honest cowhands, Bill, ordered there by that snake Buchanan."

"They made a choice, Jeb, and it was the wrong choice," the marshal averred. "They didn't have to be there, they could have refused. Even later they could have ridden away, you would have let them. But they didn't. They chose to stay and help an evil man murder a family. You might have killed them, but it was Buchanan that was responsible for their deaths, rest easy on that."

"Thanks, Bill, I'll study on that," Cassidy replied gratefully.

"Now, let's get you back to my place for something to eat and a good night's sleep. The world will look better in the morning," Yates reassured him.

Emily chimed in "Yes, let's get you home, lad," and the meeting broke up.

On the short walk to the marshal's house Cassidy suggested that the marshal might want to send out a couple of buckboards in the morning to pick up the bodies outside of town.

"Callum will have that organized and the street cleaned up before we have finished breakfast," Yates informed him. "That boy is a pure wonder for organizing."

As it happened, he proved totally correct.

Chapter 9 - Farewell

After sleeping a little late from exhaustion then consuming a hearty home-cooked breakfast, the two men strolled into the marshal's office about mid-morning to find the deputy hard at work.

"Yes, Marshal," he replied in response to Yates' inquiry. "Old Mort the undertaker has gone out with two wagons and four of the boys to pick up the bodies. He cleared Main Street last night. Jeb, your horse is down at the livery barn, and Tom Avery and the judge are waiting to talk to you in the saloon."

Cassidy thanked him and told him that he would find his pistols in his saddlebags if he would care to go and fetch them, and that he could also pick up two of the marshal's revolvers which should still be strapped to his saddle-horn.

"Talking of which," he added, "Here are your Remingtons," producing the fancy weapons from the small of his back.

"You like 'em?" Yates asked gruffly.

"Love them, they're great shooters," Cassidy stated.

"Then you keep 'em, son. A thank you gift. You will put them to better use than I could," the marshal told him generously.

"Why thank you, Bill, that is mighty kindly of you," Cassidy accepted with a wide smile.

With that the two men ambled out into the sunshine and along the boardwalk to the saloon where they found the judge and Tom Avery deep in conversation.

"Howdy, boys," the judge greeted them affably. "Tom here has been filling me in on your exploits, young man. It sounds like we are deeply indebted to you."

"No debt, Judge," Cassidy replied. "Glad to help out."

"Nonetheless, young fella, if you ever need my help in the future, you just holler," the judge offered, then handing Cassidy an envelope continued, "This here's a letter under my seal. It tells anybody in law enforcement that might want to know that I vouch for you and that they can contact me for a reference. If you need a job or are in some kind of trouble, just let them read that and I will take it from there."

Tucking the paper into the inside pocket of his leather duster the embarrassed Cassidy mumbled a sincere thank you.

Rising to his feet Avery said, "Come out back with me, Jeb, I have something to show you."

Taking the younger man by the arm Tom led him out of the rear door of the shady saloon back into the bright daylight. When Cassidy's eyes had adjusted to the glare he saw that Avery was gesturing towards a magnificent black stallion tied to a hitching ring. The horse was tall, over seventeen hands, Cassidy guessed, with a long black main and tail, hair around his fetlocks, a white star on his forehead and three white socks. His chest was deep and his neck arched proudly. He was decked out with a fancy Mexican saddle trimmed with silver conchos and a matching bridle. Altogether he was the finest piece of horseflesh that Cassidy had ever seen and he figured the beast must be worth a small fortune.

"This is Thunder," Tom Avery told him. "I raised him from a foal and he is the finest animal in my herd."

"He is really fine, Tom. You must be mighty proud of raising him," Cassidy said in a slightly awed tone.

"I am, Jeb. He's yours," Tom told him.

"What?" Cassidy exclaimed in stunned disbelief. "No, Tom, I couldn't take him. This fella must be worth a king's ransom!"

"He's yours," Avery repeated firmly. "Nothing means more to me than my family, Jeb, and I can never repay you for what you have done for us, but Thunder is the best that I can do. I will be proud to know that you are riding him."

Cassidy felt himself start to choke up and turned his face briefly away so that Tom would not see his emotions, but Tom did and he was pleased that the youngster was so taken with his gift.

"And I have spoken with Em, and we are agreed that if you ever need a home or just a place to stay you will always be welcome with us. Remember that, lad. You have a place to come home to now, where you will be treated as family," Tom finished.

"I don't know what to say<" the tough gunfighter mumbled, overcome.

"Then don't," Tom rejoined kindly, steering the young man back into the saloon. "I will have someone take him along to the livery and you and I will have a drink."

So the horse-breeder, the judge, the marshal and the gunfighter had a few sociable drinks, during which Cassidy returned his star to Yates and humorously resigned his very brief sheriff's appointment to the judge. At noon the three older men rounded up their wives and they all escorted the gunfighter to the town's only eatery, Martha's Cafe, where the other diners and Martha herself welcomed Cassidy like a hero. The food was excellent, the company jolly and it was mid-afternoon by the time Cassidy declared his intention to head out. His new friends protested vociferously but Cassidy was adamant, so Tom Avery fetched his horses and goods from the livery to the diner while the gunfighter made his round of farewells.

At the hitching rail Cassidy noticed that his chestnut had been groomed until he gleamed as brightly as Thunder, and that all his gear had been loaded onto the chestnut, leaving the black free for unencumbered riding. Taking the hint, he stepped up on to his magnificent new horse for the first time and gazed around at his new friends with a huge smile.

"I'm gonna be travelling in style now," he observed happily. Then he noticed the marshal's ten-gauge shotgun still in its saddle-boot on his chestnut. Reaching over, he jerked it loose and offered it to the marshal.

"Sorry, Bill, I forgot I still had this. It won't need cleaning, I never fired it."

"Tell you what, kid," the marshal replied. "You keep that for now; we will call it a long-term loan. See, that way you have to bring it back. And you never know, it might save your life one day. But you'll need to drop by now and again so that I know my gun's safe."

"Lordy, old man, I do believe you are beginning to like me," Cassidy kidded the marshal, grinning as he did so.

"Dream on, saddle-tramp," Yates growled gruffly back at him, fighting down a smile.

Cassidy laughed, swept his hat off in a dramatic flourish, bringing his arm down across his stomach in an extravagant mock bow from the saddle, then loped off down the street waving his hat to the assembled crowd of well wishers.

From behind he heard the marshal call "Be safe, son!"

Then, "And make sure you come back to us" in Tom Avery's voice, followed by loud cheers.

But he kept riding into the westering sun, thinking *Oh, I'll be back alright. I want to see more of Tom's gorgeous daughter.*